SHOOTING at the STARS

the Christmas Truce of 1914

JOHN HENDRIX

ABRAMS BOOKS FOR YOUNG READERS
NEW YORK

"Peace on Earth, good-will to men."

—"I Heard the Bells on Christmas Day,"
Henry Wadsworth Longfellow

One hundred years ago, a horrible war began.

It was the biggest conflict the world had ever seen. Journalists would call it the Great War, but it wasn't great at all. It was dreadful. Today, we call it the First World War.

An entire European generation was destroyed fighting a war that ultimately produced very little. Even a century later, the causes of this terrible war are identifiable, but they are dramatically insufficient considering the ghastly price of over thirty-seven million civilian and military lives. The war was built on national pride and political glory, and even more tragically, it was completely avoidable.

The war involved two opposing forces, or armies. These armies were not just a single country, but a collection of nations called an alliance. Conflict arose from the Central Powers, an alliance between Austria-Hungary, Germany, and the Ottoman Empire, now known as Turkey. The Central Powers were opposed by the Triple Entente, an alliance between France, the British Empire, and Russia. The Triple Entente eventually called for help, becoming the Allied Powers. By the end of the war the Allied and Associated Powers comprised many colonies and allies, including the United States.

The opposing forces in this massive conflict were the victims of their own alliances. Alliances were designed to prevent war by strengthening the response to an attack. But in the case of the First World War, these complex alliances actually made war more likely. They were precariously designed, like upright dominoes, and the smallest push on one country sent all the countries tumbling into war.

As the dominoes began to fall, millions of young men signed up to join the war in the late summer of 1914. Many assumed the war would be a short adventure that would certainly end by Christmas. By fall, the fighting turned nasty.

As the advances of each army stagnated, stymied by mud and new weapons like the machine gun, soldiers dug trenches in the ground to strengthen their positions. The close quarters of these battles meant that often less than one hundred feet separated opposing armies. When a bitter winter arrived on the front line in northern France, the reality of a prolonged war finally set in.

Every man on the front, no matter his uniform, was cold, fearful, and without hope of returning home anytime soon. Although these soldiers were at war and spoke different languages, the English, French, and Germans shared much—songs, faith, and a deep love of Christmas. This is the true story of what happened one cold winter evening.

France, 1914

Dearest Mother,

Thank you so much for your last Letter. Your words are a rare comfort to me in my cold trench. I so wish to make you proud and to serve my beloved England with honor... but life in this foul pit is very trying. Was I really finishing school only a few months ago? We've been stuck in the same spot since October. They say it may start raining again tomorrow.

German Line

Rain means more mud.

The mud here is like none I've ever experienced. When it rains, a thick, loamy foam churns up from the ground and fouls everything we own. The mud I remember from our garden is beautiful in comparison to this wretched stuff. It is sticky and heavy — in some places it is three feet deep! I'm not sure how anyone could fight a war in these conditions. We spend most of our time and energy trying to stay dry and warm.

When the artillery finally stops for the evening, it is time to fight the rats for dinner — which is usually cold beans. The only place to eat and sleep is in the bunkers, but when it rains, being inside is miserable.

Bunker →

It is very cold today, and clearly our hopes of the war ending by Christmas have faded. But, Mother, I must tell you about something that happened today. A tale so wonderful that you will hardly believe my account! Christmas Eve was quieter on the line than usual, and we all hoped for a day without shelling. The drastic cold that rolled in two days ago became an unexpected blessing. The hard frost turned our mucky trench back into solid ground. We had a few hours of sure-footed steps around our meager home.

After the sun went down, we decided to chance a fire outside the bunker, but when we stepped outdoors we heard the sounds of singing! I looked down the line to find out who was foolish enough to give away his position to the enemy. But the noise wasn't coming from our trench at all.

As I cautiously stuck my head over the edge of the trench, I couldn't believe what I saw!

The Germans! Our enemy was singing?

Not only were they singing as loud as they could—it sounded like "Silent Night"—but all along their line, tiny Christmas trees lit with candles and lanterns had appeared. Several of our boys suggested taking shots at the trees, but most of us were just glad the Germans weren't trying to shoot us. We wondered where they got all those little trees!

einsam wacht...

We went to sleep astonished. Fritz (that's what we always call the Germans) sang all night, it seemed. But this was nothing compared to what today would hold.

Once the sun got over the horizon, we saw the Germans hoist up a banner (on the back of an ammunition crate, I think) that said "Merry Christmas." Then came a voice—

Hallo? English Soldiers....

WHERE ARE YOUR Christmas Trees?

—followed by great laughter from their trench. We could hear everything, for they are only thirty steps to the east.

17

Rifleman Tapp, who has a great arm, took several cans of pear jam and heaved them into No Man's Land (the open ground between the trenches), very near the German line. One of their officers poked his head up, saw the jam, and then stood right up, waving at us! He wanted us to come up as well! Most of us thought it was surely a trap. But before we could do a thing, our Lieutenant Lovell had made his way through the barbed wire and was walking right out to meet the German officer!

They met and shook hands. Perhaps an angel of the Lord was among us today—what else could create such spontaneous peace but the hand of God himself?

The lieutenant signaled for us to come out. I didn't know what was happening, but it wasn't war! For one glorious Christmas morning, war had taken a holiday.

We all met along a small ditch in the center of No Man's Land. The first thing we did was bury our fellow soldiers who had been killed. They were everywhere at our feet.

It took some time to finish the grim task. I helped a German officer bury a very young soldier—he was about my age. We lashed together some crosses, and our second lieutenant, Graham Collins, said a short prayer. Then we all shook hands and wished one another a Merry Christmas.

I can hardly describe to you what it was like here. We were talking with
men we were trying to kill just the day before! A few of the lads had brought
pocket cameras from home, so they took pictures together.

I traded buttons from my field coat for a belt
buckle with a German soldier named Karl.

There was also much trading of biscuits and puddings—we had our fill. There were two soldiers in such a good mood they started kicking around an old biscuit tin like a football, using two battered tree stumps as a goal. Karl said to me,

WHY can'T
We JUST GO
Home – anD
Have PEACe?

We spent most of the afternoon out there. Mother, it was such a beautiful day.

As the evening came, we made our way back to the trenches. Many returned with souvenirs like I did. Everyone was jealous of Bruce Coy, who traded his hat for a German helmet with a pointy top—they call them "Pickelhaubes." We sat up on the edge of our trench and laughed together. It felt like I was back at school.

No sooner had we got back than Major Walter Watts came bounding in from the rear trench headquarters. He was furious and ordered us to load our weapons and be ready to fire on the German trench when he returned. He said we had acted like traitors to Britain—but how could a day of peace be treason?

The major was angry that we had befriended the enemy. They didn't seem like the enemy today.

Altogether, it was a splendid day with our foes. Tomorrow, I suppose we will all fight for our countries. And when the major returns, we will have to follow his orders. But I suspect our side will spend the rest of the night aiming high above their trench, shooting at the stars.

Merry Christmas, Mum.

With Love,
Charlie
December 25, 1914

Good night,

Author's Note

Although *Shooting at the Stars* is a fictionalized telling of the Christmas Truce of 1914, the events described are very real. Charlie's descriptions come from letters and interviews with actual soldiers who were there that day. On December 25, 1914, along many miles of the trench lines near the Belgium-France border, pockets of British, French, and German soldiers spontaneously stopped fighting and celebrated Christmas together.

Telling the story of any war is no simple task, but the narrative of the First World War is particularly fractured, complicated, and unsatisfying. Charlie's account of the Christmas Truce does not shed much light on the causes and ultimate outcomes of the Great War. But this story serves a much smaller purpose. What interests me is the point of view of the powerless. Millions of men on both sides, isolated from the grand forces of alliances and politics, were ruthlessly caught up in the wheels of war.

When I was fourteen years old, I read *All Quiet on the Western Front*, by Erich Maria Remarque, a German veteran of the Great War. I was haunted by this fictional story of Paul Bäumer, a young German man very much like myself, creative and passionate, who was stuck in a terrible war. Though he was motivated by patriotism and a youthful desire for adventure, his war changed when he mortally wounded a French soldier in No Man's Land. Paul comforted the injured soldier during the cold night as he died. To Paul, his death felt worthless.

Just as Remarque had in his tale of Paul Bäumer, I wanted to tell the story of this terrible war not from the distance of historical dates and famous battles, but from the eyes of one living it. The story of the Christmas Truce is not about politics, but people. For the trenches were not occupied by government leaders, generals, and politicians, but by masons, teachers, farmers, and other common folk. Regardless of their uniforms, the men on both sides of No Man's Land actually fighting the war were frightened, weary, and freezing. And for one bright Christmas Day, they chose to value their shared humanity over their patriotic duty.

Sadly, this moment came very early in a war that continued for four long years. The event might have been a real opportunity for a broader, lasting truce, but it was not appreciated by the commanding officers behind the front lines. In 1915, there were small attempts at another truce on Christmas (resulting in several courts-martial on the British side), but most of the men in the trenches had lost hope after a year of horror. And that same year, British commanders, embarrassed by the truce of 1914, gave direct orders to shoot any Germans above their trenches on Christmas

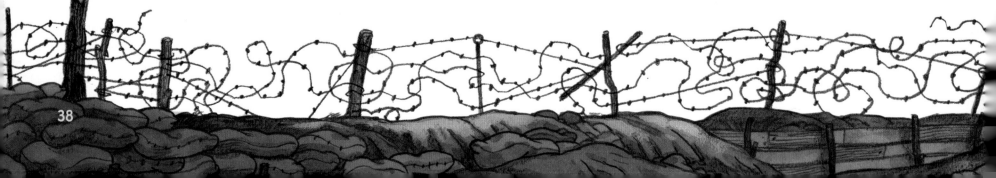

Day. Christmas trees that were set up were hit with machine-gun fire and grenades.

The remarkable Christmas Truce of the First World War stands as a lasting example of ordinary men doing the extraordinary. One English soldier, Wilfred Ewart, described it this way: "The supreme craving of humanity, the irresistible, spontaneous impulse born of a common faith and a common fear, fully triumph." Armed with carols and Christmas trees, individual men threw away their weapons and walked toward the enemy with a desperate hunger for peace.

"A friendly chat with the enemy," Christmas Truce, photograph, 1914.

Glossary

alliance A group of countries that have agreed to protect one another during wartime and cooperate in response to a crisis.

allies Two or more countries that become official friends or partners, often by signing a treaty (a mutual agreement to share goals and resources).

artillery Large weapons, like cannons and mortars, that are placed behind the front lines. These guns are too large for individual soldiers to carry into battle.

biscuit The British expression for "cookie."

bunker A protective underground shelter built into a trench network.

court-martial A committee of military officers that renders judgment for soldier disobedience; the process of facing military discipline.

football The name for the game of soccer used outside the United States; the soccer ball itself.

Fritz British slang for German soldiers. (Abbreviated from Frederick III, emperor of Germany in the nineteenth century.)

front line The dividing line between opposing armies.

lieutenant A rank in the British army, below a captain and above a second lieutenant.

loamy An adjective describing dirt that is rich and thick.

machine gun A gun that fires bullets very rapidly without pausing between rounds.

major A rank in the British army, below a colonel and above a captain.

No Man's Land An area of land between opposing trenches that is unclaimed by either side.

Pickelhaube A military helmet with a distinctive spike on the top, worn by some German forces.

rifleman A general term to describe an infantry soldier, or foot soldier.

traitor A person who betrays his country by joining or assisting enemy forces.

treason The act of betraying one's country by joining or assisting enemy forces.

trench An intricate system of ditches dug by soldiers to provide protection from enemy fire and artillery.

truce A mutual agreement to end fighting for a set period of time.

Bibliography

Brown, Malcolm, and Shirley Seaton. *Christmas Truce: The Western Front, December 1914*. London: Pan, 2001. First published in 1984 by Leo Cooper.
Murphy, Jim. *Truce: The Day the Soldiers Stopped Fighting*. New York: Scholastic, 2009.
Remarque, Erich Maria. *All Quiet on the Western Front*. Boston: Little, Brown, 1929.
Weintraub, Stanley. *Silent Night: The Story of the World War I Christmas Truce*. New York: Penguin Books/Simon & Schuster, 2002. First published in 2001 by the Free Press.

Index

To my mother, a kind and creative soul who gave me an early love of Christmas

The illustrations in this book were drawn with graphite, fluid acrylic washes and gouache on Strathmore Vellum Bristol.

Library of Congress Cataloging-in-Publication Data
Hendrix, John, 1976–
   Shooting at the stars : the Christmas truce of 1914 / John Hendrix.
      pages cm
   Summary: In 1914 France, a British soldier writes to his mother about the strange events of Christmas Eve and Christmas Day, when German and Allied soldiers met on neutral ground to share songs, food, and fun. Includes historical notes and glossary.
   Includes bibliographical references.
   ISBN 978-1-4197-1175-6 (alk. paper)
   1. Christmas Truce, 1914—Juvenile fiction.
   2. World War, 1914–1918—Juvenile fiction. [1. Christmas Truce, 1914—Fiction. 2. World War, 1914–1918—Fiction. 3. Soldiers—Fiction.] I. Title.
   PZ7.H38578Sho 2014
   [E]—dc23
   2013029535

Text and illustrations copyright © 2014 John Hendrix
Book design by Chad W. Beckerman & John Hendrix

Photograph on page 39 copyright © National Army Museum, London, Enland

Published in 2014 by Abrams Books for Young Readers, an imprint of ABRAMS. All rights reserved. No portion of this book may be reproduced, stored in a retrieval system, or transmitted in any form or by any means, mechanical, electronic, photocopying, recording, or otherwise, without written permission from the publisher.

Printed and bound in China
10 9 8 7 6 5 4 3 2 1

Abrams Books for Young Readers are available at special discounts when purchased in quantity for premiums and promotions as well as fundraising or educational use. Special editions can also be created to specification. For details, contact specialsales@abramsbooks.com or the address below.

115 West 18th Street
New York, NY 10011
www.abramsbooks.com